3 Tales

of the

Cat

Books and stories by T. Lee Harris

Twenty-Seven Cents of Luck (Short)
Cat in the Middle (Short)
Sweet Water From the Rock (Short)
Muddy Waters (Short)
Winter Wonderland (Novella)

In the Miller and Peale Series
San Francisco at Night (Short)
Chicago Blues
New York Nights

In the Josh Katzen Series
Hanukkah Gelt (Short)
The Pecan Pie Affair (Short)
The Case of the Moche Rolex*

In the Sitehuti and Nefer-Djenou Bastet series
To Be a Scribe (Short)
The Scribe Vanishes (Short)
Wanting the Fish (Short)
3 Tales of the Cat (Collection)

* Coming Soon

3 Tales

of the

Cat

T. Lee Harris

Per Bastet

3 Tales of the Cat

Copyright © 2014 T. Lee Harris

Published by Per Bastet Publications LLC, P.O. Box 3023 Corydon, IN 47112
Book designed by T. Lee Harris

ISBN 978-0-9899711-2-6

Cover Art and design by T. Lee Harris

Cover painting by T. Lee Harris Based on a detail from the 19th Dynasty tomb of Ipuy and his wife Duaemmeres at Deir el-Medina

3 Tales

of the

Cat

Contents

To Be a Scribe

The small boy stopped at the roadway as if a solid barrier had risen in front of him. He turned slowly back toward the village gleaming white in the Egyptian sun. The gate to the covered main street loomed dark and cool against the shimmer of the quickly rising heat. Many villagers were already under the brightly colored cloth sunshades on the roofs of their houses, making things and performing household chores. His family's house just outside the village walls seemed strangely silent and remote this morning, almost like the tombs that studded the surrounding hillsides.

The larger boy, who had preceded him, looked back and rolled his eyes. "Papa, Hooti's going to cry again!"

The smaller boy whipped around. "I am not! Papa, make Kaha shut up!"

Khnumhotep stopped loading the fidgeting donkey and heaved an exasperated sigh. Children were blessings from the gods, but his two youngest...? He had yet to decide just *which* gods to thank. He opened his mouth, then snapped it shut as the young man holding the donkey's halter muttered: "I'd cry, too, if I were being sent off into Aunt Tiaa's clutches."

Maybe the elder ones, too. He was definitely going to have to visit Hathor's and Meretseger's shrines and put this before the goddesses themselves. According to Kiya, his wife, it was all *their* fault in the first place. If it were, he suspected Hathor. It certainly didn't square with Meretseger's epithet of She-Who-Loves-Silence. Aloud, he said, "Shut your mouth, Ramesu, or your mother will have something to say about insulting her sister." Turning to his youngest he called out: "Sitehuti, come here."

Shooting venomous glares at Kaha, Sitehuti stomped to his father's side.

Khnumhotep placed a comforting hand on the boy's shoulder. Such a tiny one to be going to live so far away, but he was seven and many who left for school were even younger. "There's no shame in emotion, Hooti."

"I wasn't crying, Papa. I was just . . . looking . . . really."

"No one will blame you if you do. It isn't easy to leave home. It sounds hollow right now, but later, you'll be grateful for the opportunity. You owe Master Scribe Ramose a great deal for what he's taught you and to Kenhirkhopeshef for arranging this apprenticeship."

"Yes, Papa." Although he kept his face solemn, Sitehuti's mind was racing. A scribe! He was going to be a *real* scribe. And here he'd thought Ramose's adopted son didn't like him!

His father's voice intruded into his excitement. "Hooti, the Vizier's scribe is finishing his business in the Great Place today and he's offered to take you to the capital with him on his boat."

His son's eyes glowed with suppressed anticipation at the news. At least he wasn't snuffling; he also wasn't listening very well, but what seven-year-old did? "Pay attention, now, you still have to be responsible for your own things."

"Yes, Papa."

"All right, this big chest and all that's in it is your apprenticeship fee to Master Khenemetamun pa-sheri. Keep your eye on this one, because it's probably the most important one."

At his son's grave nod, Khnumhotep moved to the opposite side of the donkey. "These two smaller ones and the bundle are yours. There are gifts in one of the small ones for your Aunt Tiaa and Uncle Ptahetep to thank them being good enough to give you lodging during your schooling. The bundle has your clean. . . ."

"Look!" Ramesu's awed exclamation made his father look up. The young man was pointing back toward the village. "The Master Scribe, himself, is coming! I thought he was too sick to be out of bed."

Sitehuti wheeled toward the small procession of the aged Master Scribe in his carry-chair flanked by a fan-bearing servant on one side and Kenhirkhopeshef on the other. With a cry of delight, the boy bolted for the approaching group.

Khnumhotep grunted assent to his eldest's comment. "That's certainly what the priest of Sekhmet said yesterday."

The hurtling boy remembered himself as he neared the litter and slowed enough to bow low upon reaching his teacher's side. "My heart rejoices that my lord has come on this day!"

The old man worked hard not to chuckle out loud. "Good morning, young man, you didn't think I could let you depart without me, did you?"

The boy beamed and completely missed the dark scowl that crossed the face of the wiry young man standing in the shadow of the Master Scribe's canopy.

Kenhirkhopeshef quickly schooled his face to neutrality as he watched the exchange. In a matter of hours, the little splinter would be removed and safely on his way down river. It couldn't happen soon enough. Not that the issue of his succession to the post of Chief Scribe of the Place of Truth was in doubt. It was, after all, part of the contract struck when Ramose and Wia adopted him. The boy was simply an irritant and in the absence of grandchildren, the old man doted on him to excess. Even the way the little blister had come to the Master Scribe's attention was annoying. He and Ramose had been supervising the inscriptions being marked on a noble's canopic jar by the Chief Draftsman, Hori. It had been a beautiful day and Ramose was napping in his chair undisturbed by a group of children at play nearby. No one paid particular notice when one of the smaller boys broke away and came to watch the spells being inked in. No one noticed, that is, until the little wretch piped up: "Master Hori! You left something out, that pointy-wavy thing that goes right under the rabbit."

After a moment of stunned silence, Hori drew back to deal the boy a solid (And in Kenhirkhopeshef's opinion, much-deserved) smack when old Ramose roused himself. "The boy's right, Hori, you never could keep that straight."

To make matters worse, the old man further encouraged the boy by taking him as a *student!* Certainly the child was old enough and the gods knew he was a quick study with a knack for languages, but he was sadly lacking in decorum.

He'd about given up hope when Ramose mentioned that the boy would soon need more training than he had time or strength for. Kenhirkhopeshef had leapt to offer a letter of inquiry with his old instructor who was now an important scribe in the King's city. He'd been happily astounded when Master Khenemetamun-pa-sheri agreed to take on the new student. If that stern master couldn't beat some respect into the brat, it was hopeless. Of course, there was a risk in sending such a talent into close proximity to the royal court of the divine king Ramesses II, but still, better there than here. The junior scribe's attention was drawn by the commotion of a new group of arrivals. The boy's mother and two sisters. If this kept up, the whole village would be joining them for the trek to the river.

Kiya's face was puffy from tears as she hung a woven reed basket over her baby's shoulder. "I brought you some extra food, sweetheart. Best to be prepared, you never know what kind of things you'll find while going down river."

Khnumhotep suppressed a groan. His wife had never been farther outside the village than across the river to Thebes, still she harbored a deep suspicion that no one knew how to cook anywhere else. He checked the donkey's load a final time. "Looks like we're all here now, we better get moving."

Sitehuti stole another glance over his shoulder at the home he was leaving. Ramose saw the move from his vantage in the carry-chair and motioned to the fan-bearer who lifted the boy into the litter with his old master. "Ride with me, Sitehuti, and we can practice the proper way for you to address and thank, Amennakht, the Vizier's scribe so you will be perfect when we get to the boat."

It worked well. The boy was too absorbed to notice the village grow smaller and finally disappear behind the rocky hills.

The small dock was the busiest Sitehuti had ever seen it. The Vizier's scribe's party was just getting their luggage stowed on board and the boy's jaw dropped in awe of the vessel. It was by far the finest boat he'd ever seen, much less been on board of; big and sleek with a beautifully painted lotus flower on the bow that bent gracefully back toward the captain's perch. It had three cabins all with brightly colored woven matting for the walls and window coverings. Even the sail was beautiful, with borders of scarlet and blue against the shining white linen middle. He was still gaping when he stepped out of the litter. Ramose had to call his name twice to get his attention.

"Sitehuti, I believe you are destined for great things. The village and I have prepared a gift for you commensurate with our hopes for you." The old man rummaged under his cushions and pulled out a fine linen bag that he handed to the boy. It was heavy and solid in his hands. "Open it."

Nervously, the boy untied the bag and peeked, then pulled the object out with reverence. It was a writing kit. Turning the aromatic wooden box in his hands, he recognized the work of several of the finest village craftsmen in the delicate carvings on the sides and top. Sliding back the lid, he gasped. It held not only the standard black and red ink cakes in generous oval pans, but equally large cakes of blue, yellow and orange as well as five smaller pans of white pigment. "An illustrator's kit!"

Ramose smiled broadly. "For when your drawing hand becomes as refined as your grandfather's – I have no doubt that it will."

A deeper voice spoke behind them. "A beautiful kit, young man, and a testament to the confidence your people have in you."

Sitehuti looked toward the speaker and found a tall, spare man with sharp features standing directly behind him. The Vizier's scribe. He recognized the great man from glimpses he and the other village children had stolen as Kenhirkhopeshef had guided him around the Place of Truth where the divine kings of the past had their houses of eternity. Before he could muster words, the man spoke over his head to Master Ramose. "It gives me great pleasure to see you out and about, Master Ramose. I trust you are feeling better."

"Good day, Master Amennakht, I couldn't let my prize pupil get away without seeing him off, could I?"

Amennakht shot the old man a grin. "Of course not! I promise to take good care of him until I deliver him to his family at the capital." He looked down at the awe-struck boy. "We'd better get a move on. All the luggage has been stowed and Captain Tjety gets cranky when kept waiting."

He guided the boy away and onto the waiting boat amidst a flurry of hugs, kisses and good-byes before anyone – even Sitehuti – realized he had never delivered the greeting he'd been practicing all the way from the village.

As they stepped up onto the deck, the river breeze ruffled a ragged scrap of fur draped across the roof of the main cabin just in front of the luggage. The boy eyed it, and being unable to make sense of it, asked: "What's that?"

"That's the captain's cat."

"Is it dead?" As if in answer, the scrap of fur raised its head and surveyed the newcomer with one brassy eye, the other being long-missing – same as half of his left ear, all of his right ear and most of his fur.

The elder scribe laughed. "Not hardly! He came aboard when we were tallying grain a while back and just didn't leave. Captain Tjety adopted him. We call him Miw."

Miw stood and stretched, then dropped to the deck and sauntered over for a closer inspection that quickly zeroed in on the woven bag hanging from the boy's shoulder. "Oh, he smells the food my mother sent. Bet there's dried fish in there – usually is."

"A friend for life – or at least as long as the fish holds out!"

Just then the captain, on his perch, sounding pole at the ready, gave the order to move out. With a final wave to his family and friends on shore, Sitehuti ducked into the main cabin with the Vizier's scribe. The cat followed close on their heels.

Sitehuti was surprised that they didn't go straight to the capital, but Amennakht explained that part of his duties were to stop at various cities and deliver messages for his master, the Vizier, and sometimes even for the king, himself. At first, this was very exciting, but it soon became clear that a little boy wasn't needed on these trips ashore. Instead, Sitehuti was left in the main cabin, where Amennakht slept and the valuable items were stored, with a pile of potsherds and limestone flakes practicing his hand on classical texts. Unfortunately, Amennakht didn't have many of them committed to memory, so the story of the *Eloquent Peasant* turned up with nauseating regularity in these exercises.

It turned up again when they stopped at Khemnu, the city most sacred to the god, Thoth. Since this was also the city most sacred to scribes, he'd hoped to be permitted to go ashore, too. No luck. It was king's business and Sitehuti was again left with his pile of potsherds and the dread Peasant with only the cat for company.

"I tell you, Miw, I don't think this peasant was so eloquent. Sounds more like a whiner to me."

The cat's response was to devour one of the last pieces of dried fish from the food bag. Sitehuti sighed. "You're right, this isn't getting me anywhere. Although. . . ." He held his limestone chip out beside the copy page. His schoolboy letters looked round and irregular compared to the elegant, spiky hand of Amennakht. "I think I'm getting better, don't you?"

The cat sneezed and rooted in the food bag for another morsel.

"Me, neither."

He bent to pick up another practice piece and froze mid-reach as a seemingly disembodied hand groped past his stack of shards and scrabbled at the floor mats. Stunned, he and the cat watched as a second one slid beneath the wall mat. Both hands scrabbled for purchase against the rush flooring. Miw bristled and growled. Impulsively, Sitehuti snatched up his new writing kit, lying open beside him, and brought it down hard on the grasping intruders.

There was a strangled yelp from outside followed by a splash. He caught his breath as a voice rasped: "You clumsy idiot, you nearly took me with you."

A second voice sounded: "Wasn't my fault, Paneb. Something in there *bit* me!"

He'd heard enough. Quietly, Sitehuti edged for the door. If he could get out on deck, he could yell for help. Some of the crew were always around. . . .

He was just short of the door latch when the wall mat hiked up and a scruffy man slid partway through. Their eyes met and the boy dived for the door, but the man's reach was longer. He grabbed an ankle and pulled, hoisting himself up and dragging Sitehuti over to him in one move. A dirty hand clamped over the boy's mouth cutting off a cry of fear. His captor paused for one breathless moment, listening to see if the struggle had drawn attention from the deck. The silence was broken only by the slap of the river against the boat and the near-continual growls of Miw who was backed tightly against the big, sealed chest by the bed.

A second, wetter head, poked under the wall mat. Sitehuti's captor stood, dragging the boy with him so that his feet dangled above the matting. "Found what bit you, Kiki."

The one called Kiki advanced menacingly. "Well, well, not so vacant after all, eh, Paneb? This must be the brat they're hauling off to school. I'll teach you. . . ."

"Stop flapping your trap and get to it. Chests are over there; Neb said some jewels went into that big white one when they stopped at Abydos. You get the stuff and I'll take care of the kid."

Kiki showed his rotting teeth in an evil grin. "Right." The hand on Sitehuti's throat tightened as the other man turned back toward the chests. Miw's growl rose to a higher pitch. Kiki poked the animal with his foot. "G'wan get outta here. . . ." The rest of the command was cut off by shrill screams as the tomcat, all claws and teeth, latched onto the foot and swarmed up the man's leg. Paneb's grip on Sitehuti loosened in surprise. The boy bit the muffling hand and kicked backward at his captor who dropped him beside his abandoned writing kit. Grabbing it again, he slammed the corner into the man's foot, adding further to the howling. Bolting for the door, he threw it open and ran straight into the captain who was sprinting across the deck. Sitehuti gasped: "Two men . . . thieves. . . ."

Captain Tjety swung the boy aside as several large crewmen pounded past and into the cabin. Another crewman peered around the door as more shouts erupted, then bolted over the side and away into town. The captain turned in surprise. "Neb? What's with him?"

Sitehuti gaped after the fugitive. "I know that name! That's who told the thieves were the jewelry was."

"He did, did he?" A nod sent two more crewmen running

after the fugitive. "Well, he won't get far. Are you all right?"

"Yes."

Just then, the mauled thief was brought out onto the deck; Captain Tjety winced at the sight. "That's more than can be said for this one."

"He kicked Miw."

"Ah! Bad move."

The cat, himself, sauntered out behind his moaning handiwork, tail aloft, then leaped onto the cabin roof and fell to bathing with a sense of a job well done.

Captain Tjety's prediction proved accurate. Soon, the fugitive was dragged back looking much the worse for wear. He and the other thieves were delivered into the mayor's keeping and very early the next day, Sitehuti was escorted to court where he had to tell his story all over again.

From then on, the captain and crew made a point of keeping the boy close at hand. Not so much as a precaution for his safety as it was that the men had decided the kid was good luck. Throughout the remainder of the voyage, Sitehuti found himself in the captain's perch, learned how to sound the depth of the river with the pole, helped haul ropes and – sat on deck practicing his hand on classic pieces. As usual, the Eloquent Peasant played a major role in these sessions. He found himself longing to be done with all this copying and for his real schooling to begin.

When they finally docked at Pi-Ramesses, the captain personally escorted him through the town to his uncle's house.

Tjety was treated as an honored guest and Uncle Ptahetep insisted he stay for dinner. The captain agreed readily and during the meal, regaled the family with the story of how brave their Sitehuti was. His uncle made approving sounds and clapped the boy on the shoulder. Aunt Tiaa, on the other hand merely muttered that all the family needed was another troublemaker and shooed Sitehuti and his two cousins, Merysobek and Ptahetepmose up to bed.

The captain's booming voice followed them as they mounted the stairs with ten-year-old Merysobek in the lead. Mery seemed fit to burst until they reached their room at the back of the house. "Is it true? Did you really foil a robbery?"

Sitehuti shrugged. "I guess so, but I didn't feel all that brave while it was happening."

Three-year-old Mose's eyes were round. "I'd have been scared."

"I was." He looked around. The day had been so hectic, it was the first opportunity Sitehuti had to get a look at the room he'd be sharing with his cousins. It was a little crowded with three beds, but still larger than the room he'd shared with his brothers back home in the village. On the whole, he liked it. He liked his cousins, too, but try as he might, he just couldn't stay awake to talk.

They started out for Master Khenemetamun-pa-sheri's house early the next morning. They made an odd procession with Uncle Ptahetep and Sitehuti in the lead and two weaver apprentices bringing up the rear with the big painted chest borne on their shoulders on two stout poles. The walk was long enough that Sitehuti had more than enough time to go from excitement to fear and back to excitement again before they turned onto the Master's street. As the gates of the scribe's house came into view, the boy stopped abruptly causing the apprentices with the chest to sidestep to avoid a collision. Unaware of the grumbling behind him, he stared up in awe. "Those are the most beautiful house gates I've ever seen! Does the Master really live here?"

"He sure does."

The boy regarded the gate for a few more moments, then nodded. "Someday, I'm going to have a house just like this."

His uncle grinned. "You'll have to work hard to get as far as Master Khenemetamun-pa-sheri has."

The Master Scribe, a thickset man with a florid complexion, came out of the house just as the porter let them into the courtyard. Uncle Ptahetep stepped forward. "Good morning, Master Scribe. I am Ptahetep, the weaver. I'm here to present my nephew, Sitehuti of Western Thebes as your new student." He motioned for the apprentices to bring the chest forward. They dropped it with a grateful thump, then at a glare from Ptahetep, opened the lid and stood aside. Sitehuti was surprised to see that several lengths of fine linen had been added to the chest's contents. He glanced at his uncle who winked at him. Khenemetamun-pa-sheri bent to examine his fee, then abruptly straightened. "We were expecting you two days ago."

The boy stammered: "Yes, sir, there were some thieves at Khemnu. . . ."

"It's of no importance. Follow me; class has already begun. I certainly hope tardiness isn't going to be a problem in the future."

As the master scribe turned back toward the house, Uncle Ptahetep shrugged. "Don't worry about it. Mery or I will be back to collect you at the end of the day. Study hard!"

Sitehuti hurried to catch up with his new teacher and followed him through the house to a garden where about twenty boys of varying ages were seated cross-legged on the ground. They were all intently writing on potsherds held against the taut linen of their kilts. Khenemetamun-pa-sheri clapped his hands for attention. "Students, we are joined by Sitehuti of Western Thebes. He will be studying with us from now on. You may continue with your lesson, now." Gesturing at a basket full of shards, he told Sitehuti: "Today we are copying a classic piece. Do you have a writing kit?"

Sitehuti held up the box Chief Scribe Ramose had given him.

"A bit ostentatious, but it'll do. Find your place." The Master strode back into the house leaving Sitehuti to pick his way to an open spot. He placed the potsherd on his knee and looked at the copy text – and blinked hard. It hadn't changed; it was still *The Eloquent Peasant*.

Sitehuti sighed and wet his brush in the communal water pot.

The Scribe Vanishes

I awoke to a woman screaming. This was, however, not unusual. Since I came to live in Pi-Ramesses, I'd shared a room with my cousin Ahmose over his widowed mother's linen shop. Aunt Tiaa was my mother's sister and that side of the family was never noted for placidity. She was in rare form and the apprentices were taking the brunt of it.

At a fresh volley, Mose and I exchanged glances. We dressed fast and ran for it. I was luckier than Mose. He worked in the shop. I'd recently landed a job in the House of Life archives at the temple of Bastet.

The temple precincts were busier than usual with everyone preparing for the big festival that was coming up. Few pharaohs had seen the thirty-year reign required to hold their first Heb-Sed. The divine Ramesses II was celebrating his second. Ten days of feasting and fun. I was looking forward to it.

As I reached the Avenue of the Sphinxes leading to the temple gates, the wind shifted bringing the scent of roasting meat with it. It was probably Nakht's heavenly honey-roasted goose. Unfortunately, it also reminded me I'd left home without breakfast. The merchant stalls with their promise of food suddenly looked very inviting.

Up ahead, the High Priest's ancient servant, Huya, hobbled out of the private quarters. He saw me, waved and picked up his pace. This was impressive given both his age and the fact he'd nearly died from a blow to the head a short time ago. Forgetting the good smells, I hurried to meet him halfway.

It wound up being more than halfway and the old man wheezed alarmingly. Leaning heavily on his stick, he glanced at the vicinity of my feet and flinched. "Ah, I see the Sacred One is with you."

By "Sacred One," he meant my companion, Nefer-Djenou-Bastet, and he said it much the same way he would say "Maddened Cobra That Spits Boiling Acid." I couldn't blame him. Neffi had only been with me for a short time and, by and large, I agreed with Huya's opinion. Neffi is – or was – a temple cat, sacred to both the goddess Bastet and the Great God, Amun; and one day not so very long before, he decided he liked me. To say it changed my life is an understatement.

The old man eyed the cat. Neffi blinked and yawned, then fell to washing his hind leg. Satisfied that no nips, scratches or unexpected wet noses were forthcoming, Huya said, "I'm glad I met you, Scribe. My master instructed me to leave a message in the House of Life that he wished to speak with you in private as soon as possible. Now I can take you to him myself."

For most junior scribes, being summoned by a High Priest was heady stuff. For me, it probably meant trouble. I wasn't expecting a tongue-lashing or anything like that. High Priest Pedibastet liked me and, because of my bond with Neffi, trusted me completely. As a result, his brother-in-law liked and trusted me, too. His brother-in-law was Crown Prince

Merenptah, heir to the throne of the Two Lands. Somehow, I'd even managed to foil a plot against the royal house. Trouble was, no one believed it had more to do with dumb luck and Neffi's uncanny sense for trouble than skill. Huya's manner warned me this was more of the same. And here I'd been planning on a nice, peaceful festival. I glared at Neffi who was bathing his butt on the walkway. "Let's go. This is probably your fault, anyway."

Pedibastet was reading in a splash of light from the garden portico. The remains of breakfast sat on a small folding table nearby. He greeted me, then greeted Neffi with a piece of bread from his breakfast plate. Neffi took the crust and leapt into the High-Priest's chair – right onto a tasseled silk cushion. I cringed. That cushion was probably the rarest and most expensive thing in the room. It was also Neffi's favorite place to sit. Now he was dropping pieces of half-chewed bread all over it.

Pedibastet chuckled and scratched the cat, who arched his back higher for more. "You're early. I didn't expect to see you for another hour."

Pedibastet scooped Neffi up, shook off the cushion and sat, plopping the big cat onto his lap as if he were a tiny kitten. Neffi's behavior with the Sem-Priest always amazed me. Now he lolled in the man's lap, front legs hanging down either side of the priest's knees, eyes closed, huge paws kneading the air in time to loud purrs. The old man fixed me with his formidable stare. "Are you ready for the festival?"

"Oh, yes, Sir! I've seen several of the three-year festivals since I came to stay in the capital. They were pretty memorable." I reflected with chagrin that some had been more memorable than others. Some post-festival mornings had been even *more* memorable, but I didn't bother the Sem Priest with that.

"You're far too young to remember the Pharaoh's first Heb-Sed, but it was a celebration like none before it. He performed all the physical feats himself in those days. The feasting and dancing went on day and night. The plans for this second look grander than the first."

"Will Prince Merenptah be standing in for the Pharaoh again?"

"Of course." Pedibastet shook his head. "You've seen him, Sitehuti. There's little of the great Ramesses left these days. He can hardly walk across his audience chamber let alone run around the Heb-Sed enclosure. A pity. You should have seen him in his prime...." He trailed off, looking beyond me into the past, deep-set eyes seeing something I could only guess at. Abruptly, he refocused on me. "Preparations for the Census of the Cattle begin tomorrow."

I perked up. Any scribe would. We played an important part in accounting the wealth of the Two Lands that began the official Heb-Sed. "I heard a rumor that my old master is to be in charge of the Census."

"The rumor is correct. Khenemetamun-pa-sheri may be an arrogant prig, but he's still one of the best scribes in the city. You were fortunate to have studied under him. He leaves today for the royal storehouses of Saqqara." He scratched Neffi under the chin. "You will be going with him."

There it was. "I'm going to be a scribe for the Census?"

"Yes and no. You're going with the scribal party for the Census, but your job is a little different. This is quite a puzzle, my boy."

"I'm not very good at puzzles, Your Eminence."

Pedibastet coughed his odd laugh. "You are too modest. If not for your ability with puzzles, there would be no great house of Ramesses today." Neffi hopped down, stretched and sauntered off. I tried to keep an eye on him and pay attention to the Sem-Priest at the same time.

"It has come to the Royal Overseer's attention through anonymous letters that valuable items are disappearing from a particular storehouse."

"This is the storehouse where the Census is to take place?" Neffi rooted for crumbs around the folding table.

"It is. Doubtless, the thievery has been going on for a while, but when items for the Heb-Sed vanish…this is not so easy to hide."

A spotted paw snaked up and fished around for more scraps from the breakfast remains. The table rocked dangerously. I sidled over and edged him away with my foot. "A thief would have to be very brazen or very foolish to think that would go unnoticed. There's more to this, isn't there, Sir?"

"Perceptive as usual, my young friend. The overseer of the storehouse is Ramesses' grandson, Heqamaatre."

It was almost as bad as I feared. The news left me holding my breath for a few heartbeats. Neffi took advantage of the pause to snatch a chunk of bread sopped in sesame paste and run for the gardens. "Ummmm . . . then I'll be conferring with him when I arrive."

"No. This investigation is being run from the palace. No need to mention this to Heqamaatre."

It *was* as bad as I feared. Pedibastet was avoiding telling me outright that the Pharaoh's grandson was under suspicion. Shouting erupted from the garden. I ignored it.

"Don't look so wary. The prince only wants you to accompany your teacher as his assistant. Look around. Ask questions. Notice things. It was fortunate he was appointed Scribe for the Census of the Cattle. No one will think twice about a former student assisting him."

"Yes, Your Eminence. Pardon me for mentioning this, but the Census takes several days. I'll need to pack. . . ."

The High-Priest cough-laughed again. "A chest containing all you'll need has already been requested from the temple stores. It will likely arrive at the school before you do."

"What if he leaves without me?"

"He's waiting for final instructions from the palace." The Sem-Priest sealed and handed me the scroll he'd been reading. "And here they are."

I did not race to my appointment on wingéd feet. I may have been fortunate to study under Khenemetamun-pa-sheri, but I counted myself doubly lucky to be out from under his thumb. Now I was right back there. Temporary or not, it wasn't a happy circumstance.

Outside, that aroma grabbed me again. It was sure to be a long day and no way did I want to face my old teacher on an empty stomach. Following my nose led me straight to Nakht's stall. Maybe I did have a little detecting skill after all.

I took my breakfast over to one of the low benches beside the shop. Ignoring the insistent rubbing at my knees, I took a bite and chewed appreciatively. It was mostly bread, but the succulent sauce had run all over it.

Someone poked me from behind and boomed, "Hurry up, kid, you're going to be late!"

The bite went down the wrong way. I was pounded on the back until the chunk of bread flew out. I whirled and found myself nose to scaled breastplate of the captain of Merenptah's Medjay guard. "Hey! Don't die with your mouth full, scribe. You can't recite the proper spells, that way."

I wiped my face. "Very funny, Djedmose. Let me guess. You've been sent to make sure I get where I'm going."

The Nubian's face split in a wicked grin. "Of course not. I'm leading the official guard for the scribal party. Just decided this morning. Finding you dawdling was a bonus."

I turned back to the table. My breakfast was gone and Neffi sat in its place, cleaning his face.

"Well, come on, then, no use hanging around here all morning." I snatched up the purring thief and slung him onto my shoulders. He complained – or maybe burped. I stomped off.

Chuckling, Djedmose caught up with me. It wasn't hard since his legs were a lot longer. "Don't get your loincloth in a knot, Scribe, I have good news. Our Anonymous isn't anymore. He's a mid-level scribe name of Sahathor. At the moment he isn't hot to point fingers, but I figure we can lean on him a little and who knows . . . ?" Djedmose's grin widened. "Looks like we're going to be busy."

I groaned.

When we got to the school, preparations were well underway for the trip to Saqqara. Scribes, servants and the escort contingent clogged the courtyard and spilled out into the street. My old master was in the main room, barking orders at scurrying students. Made me feel right at home. It took major effort to squash the urge to duck and run. I called to him over the hubbub. Khenemetamun-pa-sheri paled. I think he would have liked to slam the door in our faces and ram the bolt home. It wasn't Djedmose or me, but Neffi, who was still riding on my shoulders. Neffi and my former teacher had a long-standing animosity. Point of fact, this was the whole reason I was where I was. If he hadn't been so set on avoiding the cat, I wouldn't have been sent to the temple to take dictation from the High-Priest in his place. Come to think of it, I owed my old teacher a lot. Not all of it good.

Djedmose gave me a wink and took control of the aimlessly milling guard, shouting them into sharp order. It only took a glimpse of Merenptah's official seal on the scroll I held to convince Khenemetamun-pa-sheri to follow me into his study. There, behind closed doors, I handed over the letter. Neffi jumped off my shoulder to explore. My teacher's face was a road map of his progress through the message as he went from thinking I was simply a messenger to realizing I was included in his personal party. He glared at me over the edge of the papyrus. "So you've become a Royal spy."

"That's kind of an insulting description, Sir. I'd also like to point out that I didn't ask for this, either. It was the Crown Prince's idea and if you'd like to argue with him, I'll hold your writing kit."

He ground his teeth. "And that . . . that . . . cat demon!" It was a non-sequitur, but I couldn't fault him on that particular description, so I kept my mouth shut.

"I suppose this is why I was chosen to head the Census?"

I was aghast. "No, sir! Pedibastet, himself, told me you were chosen because you were the best scribe in the capital!"

"He said that?"

"Absolutely, Sir. Just this morning when he gave me the orders." Okay, not precisely his words, but close enough.

Mollified, he placed the letter in a bowl, poured water over it and moved it from side to side until all trace of ink was gone. "It's best this isn't read by anyone else." Suddenly, he jumped and yelped. "What's he doing over there?"

I turned and saw Neffi burrowed under a stack of papyri. He stood up, scattering scrolls and pranced over proudly holding a large beetle in his teeth. I reached for him, but he danced away. With a few crunches, his prize was gone.

My teacher's normally ruddy face took on a greenish tinge. He motioned abruptly toward the scattered scrolls, then fled the room. I shrugged and did as any good assistant would do: restacked the scrolls.

The journey to Saqqara was mercifully uneventful. Neffi, who for some odd, un-catlike reason was calmed by riding on a boat, slept in the sun most of the way. No one was more relieved at this than my master. He spent the journey making the most of having an assistant by getting in as much dictation as possible. I must have caught up his correspondence until sometime into the next year.

When our entourage disembarked at the storehouse docks, Heqamaatre and his assistant met us. The overseer had inherited the Ramessid features, but on him they looked pinched rather than commanding. That might have had something to do with the fact he was anything but happy to see us.

After the preliminary greeting to the Master Scribe, the overseer pointed past my teacher toward Captain Djedmose. "That man is the captain of my uncle's personal guard. Why do you need a Royal Medjay contingent?"

The Master Scribe smiled. "Prince Merenptah honors me by lending his elite escort to my entourage. He wishes to ensure that his father's festival and the Census go smoothly." He swept a hand toward me. "Allow me to introduce my assistant, Sitehuti of Western Thebes."

Heqamaatre regarded me down the regal length of his nose, then blinked as Neffi yawned, leapt off the boat and strolled over to sit at my feet. "That's a temple cat."

I bowed. "Yes, Excellency. I'm afraid he's taken a liking to me."

"I see." Heqamaatre nodded warily. Neffi's reputation had a bad habit of preceding him.

As assistant to the official Census scribe, it fell to me to work with Heqamaatre's own assistant, Patwere, to ready our quarters. Patwere was a wiry man, just a little taller than me and he was a chatterer.

I folded the Master Scribe's best cloak across the high bed and looked around. "Nice place! Do you live here, too?"

Patwere shook his head. "No, I have a small house in the village. Heqamaatre does well for himself, though. His family connections bring him a lot of favor – you do know he's the Pharaoh's grandson?"

"Yes, I'd heard." Neffi jumped onto the freshly folded cloak and wadded it up to make himself comfortable.

"Not that it makes much difference. There are an awful lot of grandsons. Most of the officials in the Two Lands must be related to the Royal family."

He had a point. Even before his mind began to wander, I think the great Ramesses, himself, had lost track of just how many children and grandchildren he had. I considered making Neffi get off the cloak, then decided against it. "Speaking of relations, I promised a friend I'd look up a cousin of his. A guy named Sahathor. Know him?"

Patwere rolled his eyes then caught himself. "I suppose that isn't a proper response for someone who doesn't know him – Sahathor, I mean."

I grinned. "Don't worry, my friend said his cousin was a character."

Patwere was relieved. "Oh, good. You never know what kind of face someone puts on for their relatives. It doesn't sound like you'll be surprised if I tell you Sahathor is off on one of his benders again."

"Again? I'm amazed he hasn't been sacked by now."

That was the right thing to say. It launched a monologue of gossip, suspicion and petty complaints that lasted the better part of the hour we spent unpacking. I learned that Sahathor enjoyed his drink a little too much and had a habit of disappearing for days at a time. I also found out that he wasn't called to task for it because the overseer also liked his tipple.

Patwere excused himself just before my companions returned. When I shared my news, Djedmose frowned. "Disappeared on a drunk? That's a problem. When did he go missing?"

"About two days ago. According to Patwere, he ought to be stumbling in any time now. He's rarely gone longer than three days."

Khenemetamun-pa-sheri said, "Missing for days at a time? And no one is upset about this? If it were one of my scribes, I'd be furious." He would, too. Even being late won the offender a good caning.

I shrugged. "Apparently he's Heqamaatre's drinking buddy. They frequently go missing together."

Djedmose's frown deepened. "Prince Merenptah won't be happy to hear that. Nephew or no, he expects Royal appointees to take their responsibilities seriously."

My teacher nodded. "As well he should! A lot can be . . . what's that *cat* doing on my bed?"

We all glanced at Neffi. He was on his back, sound asleep, comfortable in the crumpled embroidery of the older scribe's cloak. Stretched full length, he took up most of the bed.

Djedmose grinned. "He appears to be sleeping, Excellency. Shall I wake him?"

"No. No. No need. It's warmed considerably. I won't need a cloak."

He was wrong. When Patwere came to collect us for the walking tour of the facility, Neffi was still snoring on the cloak. Khenemetamun-pa-sheri made a brave show of being warm in the crisp afternoon sun, but nobody believed him. The goosebumps and chattering teeth were a dead giveaway.

The Census of the Cattle officially began at sunrise. I accompanied the recording party, making like a dutiful assistant until midday when my teacher told me to get lost. It was Neffi's fault, as usual. He'd taken a liking to the embroidered yoke of Khenemetamun-pa-sheri's cloak and kept climbing him to ride on his shoulders. Sort of makes legible writing difficult.

Time to do what I was there for and look around. Right. Like I knew what to look for. I put Neffi down and he wandered off. Having no better idea, I followed him. He led me into the granaries. I was awestruck by the huge hive-shaped mudbrick buildings. Such simple structures, yet they were the lifeline of the nation. Recording their contents figured prominently in the Heb-Sed.

Neffi trotted toward an empty granary, tail swishing. Soon, it would be filled one basket at a time while scribes recorded each load. I suddenly realized Neffi was on top of it now.

He clawed at the bricks, then looked down at me. "Yeow!"

"Neffi! Get down!"

He scratched harder. Bits of brick flew.

"EEEEYOOOOWWW!"

I climbed up and grabbed at him. He eluded me and dug at the other side of the hatch. "What is wrong with you? This place was cleared – even the mice are gone."

"EEEEYOWWW!"

"Leave it!"

Neffi attacked the hatch and I dived for him until finally, I growled, "All right, I'll prove it's empty!" I snatched the handle of the hatch and pulled.

The odor that hit me wasn't the aroma of past grain harvests, but I recognized it, anyway. It was one I hoped never to encounter again. I hastily dropped the lid back into place and crouched, gulping air, until Neffi's face pushed into mine. That cat has smug down pat. "Okay. So it isn't all that empty."

Lamp light cast distorted shadows on the interior of the granary as Djedmose bent low over the corpse. The man had been dead for several days and in spite of the bundles of cloves tied over our noses, we were breathing shallowly. The Medjay topside quit peeking in after the first good whiff. The only one who seemed unaffected was Neffi who was busy inspecting the edges of the floor.

The body probably hadn't been a pretty sight even before decomposition set in. The back of the head was crushed and shards of a beer jar were everywhere. Djedmose rolled the man over and grunted. "Well, kid, you get the job done fast. This is Sahathor, the guy we were supposed to find, but it looks like talking to him is out unless you know a real good magician."

I resituated my cloves. "Don't blame me; Neffi found him. I just opened the lid before he dug through the bricks."

He shot a look over his shoulder. "That cat scares me sometimes. Regardless, we have another problem on our hands. Now we have to find out who killed him."

"Maybe he fell in accidentally and . . . ?"

Djedmose just looked at me.

"Guess not."

Neffi turned his attention to the beaten earth floor where the dead man had lain. I was preparing to shoo him off, when he pounced on something embedded in the dirt and batted it across the floor. It glittered in the dim light as it skittered across the uneven surface. That got Djedmose's attention. "What's he got now?"

Retrieving the object was easier than I expected. Neffi crinkled his eyes and purred as I took it from between his paws. "It's a gold lotus blossom with turquoise insets. Looks like it's from a piece of jewelry."

"Let me see." The Nubian turned the fragment around in his hands and gave a low whistle. "Expensive. Probably from the Royal workshops." Expression unreadable in the shadows, he glanced at Neffi. "We need a chat with Heqamaatre. Grab the Sacred One."

Heqamaatre was in his office with Patwere taking inventory of recently-arrived items. The office was large, but seemed cramped due to the number of items awaiting cataloging. Patwere sat cross-legged on the floor in the traditional scribal manner using his stretched kilt to hold the papyrus. He took

one look at Djedmose's face, slid a glance at me, and hastily excused himself.

Heqamaatre was annoyed. "Captain Djedmose, what is the meaning of this? We're already behind schedule."

"Are things going slowly because of your missing scribe?"

"Yes, damn him. He's thrown everything off."

"Then you'll be interested to know we've found him. More precisely: his body. It was found in an empty granary earlier today."

The overseer sat down hard on a gilded chair. It looked more like his legs had quit than a voluntary action. "I see. I'll summon the facility's police chief, then."

"No need, Sir. My men are handling it."

Silence loomed. Djedmose was master of the silent sweat.

So far, they'd ignored me. Fine. I'd planned to let Djedmose do the talking, anyway. Neffi squirmed out of my arms and trotted over to a roll of fine linen, sniffed, then rubbed along its length.

The overseer demanded, "What's that cat doing?"

Djedmose said, "Being a cat, Sir. About Sahathor. I'm a little surprised he'd be missing for days and no one was concerned."

Neffi moved on to a large alabaster vase and stretched against it to sniff the seal covering its mouth. The vase was heavy and didn't even wobble, but Heqamaatre flinched, anyway. I quit watching Neffi and started watching the overseer. He pulled his gaze from Neffi onto Djedmose. "I'm afraid Sahathor was prone to disappearing, Captain. We all thought he'd turn up soon."

"Looks like he has."

Heqamaatre looked sick. Neffi rustled through some scrolls, sneezed, wound around the ornate legs of a folding stool, then disappeared behind a group of chests.

"You haven't asked how he died," Djedmose said.

Trilling, Neffi hopped into sight again onto the top of a large, painted chest. He lay across the lid, batting at the clay seal dangling from the binding cords. It was the Royal Seal.

Heqamaatre jumped up as if prodded with a hot coal. "Get him away from that!"

Djedmose watched Neffi with a raised eyebrow. The cat was now lying on his side pawing at the base of the box. "What's in that chest?"

"Those are items for the Heb-Sed. They haven't been recorded yet."

Neffi was purring loudly, clawing at the crack of the lid. Djedmose said, "Open it, please."

"Impossible. Those items belong to my grandfather, the Pharaoh . . . ."

"And I represent the Pharaoh. Open the box."

Heqamaatre hesitated, then bent to cut the seal. Neffi dived for the opening lid, but I saw what he was going for before he got there. Over the protests of the overseer, I lifted out a heavy gold pectoral. Its colorful stone and glass inlay glittered as I took the small lotus blossom from my writing kit and fitted it into an almost unnoticeable gap at the bottom edge.

Heqamaatre cried out, "You've broken it!"

Djedmose took the flower and held it up. "It's broken,

yes, but Sitehuti didn't do it. We found this piece under Sahathor's body. Any idea how it got there?"

All pretense of self-control fled. He crumpled back into the chair, head in hands. "So much blood. I had no idea there'd be so much blood."

Djedmose stood, head bowed, arms folded in what I recognized as his listening stance. "You better tell me what happened." He didn't have to wait long.

"It was an accident. We were drinking and . . . *why* did he write those damned letters?" Heqamaatre leaned back. "Have you ever seen the goods that come through these storehouses? It's crazy. No one can use all that. We started taking food and wine. Why not? I'm part of the Royal Family, right?

"The wine got Sahathor. He loved parties and we threw some great ones. When that got stale, we moved on to bigger items." He shrugged. "I started to enjoy it. It was thrilling to walk away with things and no one was the wiser. Sahathor wasn't like that. All the idiot wanted was to drink and party.

"Heb-Sed goods started coming in. Real nice things. I didn't see a problem with taking a few here and there. Sahathor got scared and wrote a letter to the Royal Overseer.

"I didn't know anything about that until later when we were sharing beer in one of our hideaways. We'd been drinking all day and I could tell Sahathor was nervous. Finally he told me about the letters. I told him he was a fool.

"He showed me a pectoral from our cache. Said he was going to hand it over as a token of good faith. I couldn't let that happen. I grabbed for it and we fought. He just wouldn't let *go*. Next thing I knew, the beer jug was crashing down . . . he fell and didn't move.

"I panicked and hid the necklace in a chest that just arrived and resealed it. Before I could figure out what to do next, your party arrived."

Silence reigned again. Even Neffi was still, sitting beside the coffer regarding the man with half-closed eyes. Finally Heqamaatre asked, "What happens now?"

A few days later, I stood beside Djedmose as his Medjays escorted Heqamaatre onto a boat headed back to the capital. Shoulders slumped, all haughtiness gone, he barely resembled the man who met us on the same docks such a short time before. I wasn't real happy, either.

Djedmose said, "You and the magic cat came through again, kid. Found the thief and solved a murder all at the same time."

"Then, why am I staying here while you're going home?"

"Leave while there's still work to do?" He laughed and swatted me on the back. "Not a chance. You're the assistant to the official scribe of the Census, remember?"

With that, he bounded on board and the crew pushed off. I sat down on the planking next to Neffi, who was stretched full length to absorb all possible warmth, and watched them sail away. When the boat receded far enough I could no longer make out the details of its rigging, I stood and poked Neffi with my toe. "Let's get back to work. This is all your fault, anyway."

Wanting the Fish

The fish were laughing at me. They gathered in the shadow of my papyrus boat, waiting for the next entertainment. I situated my feet on the sides of the canoe, and gripped the spear firmly – which must've twitched the attached cord, because it suddenly jerked backwards. Turning, I disengaged the cord from the teeth and claws of the large, playfully growling cat. "Neffi! Get off!" Rippling spotted fur in satisfaction, he sauntered to the back of the boat and flattened himself over the bundled stems where he watched the gathered fish, tail lashing. "Nefer-Djenou-Bastet! You have got to be the most unhelpful animal in the two lands. I'll never catch a fish if you keep doing that."

It took some effort to put the cord right, but at last, I was standing again, spear poised, reviewing the morning's instructions: Hold it firmly, but not too tightly, let the shaft be an extension of your arm, and most of all, *want* that fish!

In the distance, a shout of triumph rang out, a reminder of why I was upstream from the rest of the hunting party where only the fish laughed at me. Rekhi-mi-re, grandson of the divine Ramesses II (Life, Prosperity and Health for a million years), priest of Amun and all around fathead, had obviously speared a prize. I gritted my teeth, concentrated on the biggest, most obnoxious fish below and hove the weapon. It splashed into the water clumsily and the fish scattered.

"Sitehuti, that was the most piss-poor spear throw I've

ever witnessed. If you were in the army, you wouldn't be for long."

I looked toward the riverbank where the shout originated. Djedmose, captain of Crown Prince Merenptah's Medjay contingent stood there, arms folded, grinning. I reeled in my empty fishing spear. "Then it's a good thing I'm not a soldier, isn't it? I seem to be constantly reminding people I'm a scribe, not what they think I ought to be."

He laughed. "Well, you win your argument for not being a fisherman."

"If you want a fish written about or drawn and painted, I'm your man. If you want one caught—" My tirade was interrupted by a splash and sudden flopping in the bottom of the boat. Glancing around in surprise I found Neffi licking a

wet paw standing over a large fish thrashing against the papyrus.

"—you'll have your magic cat do it." If Djedmose's grin had gotten any wider, the top of his head would have fallen off.

I fumbled the oar-pole; it splashed into the water and drifted out of reach. Angrily, I snatched the spear and used it to pole the boat to shore.

The Nubian hauled me in with insulting ease and took possession of the weapon. "Where's the boy who was supposed to be steering your boat?"

I glared at Neffi, who purred and headbutted my leg. Djedmose followed my gaze and chuckled. "The Sacred One again?" He flung the spear out, deftly snared the errant pole and reeled them both in, his face clouding slightly. "Regardless, that boy'll get a hiding for leaving you. It's not safe to be out here alone. There are hippos just down river and Si-Montu says he heard a crocodile chuffing this morning."

"I so love the outdoors." Raucous shouts and laughter echoed back to us. "Remind me why I'm here again."

Some of the Medjay's good humor returned. He mimicked his deepest court bow. "It is a reward for services rendered to the royal house, O most-favored Sitehuti of Western Thebes — Life, Prosperity and Health to you!" He laughed and straightened. "Most courtiers would kill to be where you are."

Courtier. Every scribe dreamed of being a courtier. I did too, but it had always involved working toward it by transcribing letters and documents of state. Somehow, I'd achieved it before even graduating scribal school simply by being adopted by a cat. Granted, Nefer-Djenou-Bastet was special, even for a temple cat. His markings linked him to the great guardian cat of Re as well as being sacred to Bastet, herself. When he chose me to be his companion, the High Priest of the temple, Pedibastet (who was also the brother-in-law of the crown prince) decided that made me special, too, which changed my life in ways that never entered my dreams.

Captain Djedmose of the Royal Medjay was one of those ways. When we first met, he'd been sent to my Master's house to escort me into the presence of Crown Prince Merenptah. At the time I'd thought he was going to kill me. So did he. Instead, we ended up working together, much to his irritation.

I wasn't real happy about it either, but for different reasons. The Royal house of Userma'atre Setepenre Ramesses Meriamon had problems and it seemed evident to everyone but me, that I'd been tapped by the gods themselves to unravel them. That was Neffi's fault. It's *always* Neffi's fault. At least he'd come through each time and pointed the way to the solution. I'd be dead several times over if he hadn't.

Djedmose had a hand in saving my sorry skin on multiple occasions, too. Oddly enough, that seemed to change his attitude greatly. He originally saw Neffi as a stupid animal his superiors were reading too much into and me as a social-climbing wannabe aristocrat. He now viewed Neffi with a type of respect and me as a sort of troublesome younger brother. That worked for me. I was the youngest of my siblings; I was used to being treated that way. I was trading on that attitude when I turned back to him. "Not to sound ungrateful, but what was wrong with a nice gold necklace?"

"Anyone can have a gold necklace, Scribe. His Highness, Merenptah, and his Eminence, Pedibastet, wanted to give you something special. You know how they both love hunting and fishing. They hoped you would enjoy it, too."

"Guess I'm just not the rugged type." More shouting and hooting echoed from the camp. I grimaced. "Sounds more like a troupe of baboons than the flower of aristocracy."

Djedmose nodded. "They been giving you a hard time, I know. Have to expect that, though. You're the new kid."

"I have to expect it, but I don't have to sit there and take it. All due respect to the king and crown prince, but the more distance I can put between prince Rekhi-mi-re and myself the better. He probably feels the same."

Djedmose laughed sourly. "You're right, there. He seems to view you as a rival. Senseless, really. Even if you wanted a priesthood, it isn't like they're in short supply. It doesn't help that it's his own grandfather through his uncle who is bestowing honors on you." He paused in looping the javelin's return line. "If you want the truth, he's not the one who worries me. It's that friend of his, Setnacht. That boy is just reckless. Been talking about going after the hippos himself ever since he overheard Si-Montu telling me about them."

"That's not reckless, that's insane!"

Djedmose gave me a startled look.

I couldn't suppress a shudder. "Hey, I didn't see much hunting growing up in the desert at the Place of Truth, but I did see a couple of ritual hippopotamus hunts. I was young, but the memory of those huge, angry animals charging barges is very vivid. Terrified me. Gave me nightmares for months."

"Too true, Scribe. I've seen my share of hunts and participated in a few. Hippos do not go down as easily as that fool thinks." He shot me an assessing glance. "The workers' village is pretty far from the river. Where this bunch played with throwing sticks, you probably cut your teeth on craftsman's tools."

It was my turn to laugh. "By the time I was three, I could put a fine enough point on a brush, the senior draftsmen would borrow me for important projects. Then, I came to the capital and began my apprenticeship with Master Khenemetamun-pa-sheri. Hunting and spear fishing were not in the curriculum."

"We'll have to fix that, won't we?" He handed me the spear. "Okay, your stance is pretty good. We need to work on delivery, though."

We practiced spear throws until the sun sank toward the western horizon. Even with the added encouragement of a revolving number of Medjay who joined us throughout the day, I never landed a single fish. Neffi caught three more.

Djedmose shook his head and lifted the string of fish. "We'd better head back to camp. It'll be dark soon and we need to get these guys to the cooks."

The soldiers bantered about my grip and follow-through all the way back until my head was swimming like a fish. When we reached the pavilions, the cook's assistant whisked the string from Djedmose and hurried away. Rekhi-mi-re snagged the boy as he dashed by and examined the catch, then roared over his shoulder: "Ha! It appears the magic cat caught more fish than you, Setnacht!"

The other noblemen laughed and Setnacht fixed me with

a dark glare. He was a minor priest at the same temple as Rekhi-mi-re and had viewed my inclusion into the camping trip with overt hostility from the start. "At least I speared my own. Did you ever figure out which end of the spear was for the fish, Sitehuti?"

Another minor priest snorted into his wine cup. "Don't be so hard on the kid, Seti. Maybe they club fish to death in the backwater he comes from."

Still another jibed: "They must talk them to death where you come from, Un'e, but the ones here weren't listening." Laughter erupted and the conversation thankfully veered away from me and my hunting skills – or lack thereof.

During the meal, I realized Djedmose was watching me. He always became quieter and more formal the closer we came to the camp, but in the firelight, he ventured a wink at me. "We'll work on that follow-through again tomorrow."

I sighed and accepted a cup of wine offered by the camp steward. "It isn't so much my follow-through, I think I just don't *want* the fish that much."

Captain Djedmose was overtaken with a coughing fit that necessitated a big gulp of beer.

I excused myself, scooped up a drowsy Neffi and headed for my tent as soon as I could. This was in part because of the unpleasantness of my dinner companions, but mostly because my pavilion and camp furniture were the only part of this outing I liked.

As I stepped inside and let the curtain fall behind me, the baboons at the fire seemed to recede. It was purely in my imagination. The fabric of the tent walls wasn't that heavy, but with it closed, I was in another world.

When the High Priest, Pedibastet, announced my reward to me, he had mistaken my look of panic to mean "oh no, and me with no camping equipment" instead of just plain "oh no". He immediately assured me that one of his old sets had been prepared for my use. He kept stressing that it was an old set, so no need to be extra careful. I doubted he was even remotely aware that his old and used was better than what I lived with every day. I felt like a prince, myself, inside that tent.

The steward had anticipated me. He'd breezed through like an Ifrit, leaving in his wake a lit lamp, a basin of clean water on the small table and a turned down bed. Neffi wriggled out of my grasp to inspect the bed linens and I had a quick wash, then put the bowl on the floor by a folding chair. Kicking off my sandals, I sank back into the chair and plunked my bare feet into the basin. My feet had been in water most of the day, but this water had the benefit of being wonderfully siltless. I was in danger of falling asleep in the chair. I levered myself up, wandered over to the ingeniously designed camp bed, dislodged Neffi and climbed in. The crisp linen bedding felt glorious and the string webbing below gave just enough. I remember wondering as I drifted off if the Sem-Priest would notice if I didn't return the bed.

The next day we went duck hunting. My skill with a throwing stick was, if possible, worse than my skill with a fishing spear. Neffi, however, proved as adept at catching birds as fish. Maybe a little more so. During the day he brought me two geese and four ducks. Unfortunately, he steadfastly refused to retrieve my throw stick, so I had to go find it myself. The things are curved and are supposed to return to the thrower, but mine seemed to have a mind of its own. It went everywhere but back to me. I take that back. There was the one time it returned to whack me between the shoulder blades. To give the Medjay credit, they didn't laugh – much. I did learn a whole new vocabulary of Nubian swearwords when the stick hit them, though.

From time to time, I caught Djedmose grimacing at my throws and sensed the onset of another hunting tutorial. I was right. We tossed sticks at targets until the light got too bad to see where the weapons landed, which, to the credit of my instructor, was closer to the mark by the end of the day. Still, I was bone-tired and longing for my bed when we dragged back into camp. The aroma of roasted goose woke me a little and drew both Djedmose and myself toward the circle around the brazier.

At our approach, Setnacht stood and violently poked the fire with a stick. It was burning quite well, so the action was unnecessary and inexplicable. Inexplicable, that is, until Rekhi-mi-re laughed and turned to me. "Sitehuti, your magic cat is the author of tonight's feast. The two geese he brought down were the best catch of the day."

Un'e snickered. "For those of us who caught anything."

It soon became apparent from the conversation that Setnacht had no luck with his throw stick. These scions of the noble houses weren't any nicer to people they liked than they were to those they didn't. Unfortunately, Setnacht appeared to be the type who could dish it out but not take it and the jibes were putting him in a dangerously bad mood.

I was wondering where the breaking point would be, when

the night was cut by the bellow of a hippopotamus. Conversation stopped and one of the Medjay shifted uncomfortably. "That's awfully close, Captain."

Djedmose's eyes glittered in the firelight as he nodded curtly. "Too close. We better move the camp tomorrow."

Setnacht shook his head. "We're hunters. We should go after it."

"NO. No one is to go after that hippo."

Rekhi-mi-re swiveled on his stool and fixed the Nubian with a glare. "That sounded like an order, Captain. Who are you to give us orders?"

Djedmose folded his arms across his chest. "I'm the man your grandfather charged with keeping you safe, Highness."

Setnacht smacked a fist onto his thigh. "It's ridiculous to move the camp. After all, it's just an animal. My father has killed several hippos."

Djedmose spoke slowly and deliberately. "A hippopotamus is not just an animal, Sir. They are fast, tough and dangerous when angered. There's a reason they're the avatar of Set."

The cook and his assistants charged into the tension with the roasted geese and fresh bread. Brave men. I'm not sure I'd have done it. Regardless, everyone fell to the business of eating and no one mentioned the hippopotamus again. I did notice Djedmose having a quiet word with his men, though.

🐾 🐾 🐾

"It will be a contest." Murmurs of interest greeted Rekhi-mi-re's announcement after breakfast. "We're going to fish again and whoever brings in the biggest catch wins a jug of the excellent white wine from my family vineyards."

The other nobles greeted the prize named with a great deal of enthusiasm and they dispersed very quickly to find the best spots. Oddly enough, the Medjay also melted into the reeds, swiftly and silently until only Djedmose, his lieutenant Si-Montu and I were left on the riverbank. Djedmose grinned at me. "You'd better find your spot, too, Scribe."

I snorted, and sat back down for another chunk of date bread.

I spent the morning fishing in the shallows right by the camp. I had no hope of catching anything anyway, so I figured to stay close to home since the others were gone. All in all, it was an enjoyable few hours. I got in some passable spear throwing practice and chatted with the steward and cooks while Neffi pounced on things nearby. He didn't go too far away, but this was mostly because the cooks kept slipping him tidbits as they prepared the midday meal. They were roasting Neffi's ducks and doing something very interesting with honey and spices.

The others must have been drawn by the aromas, too, because they all began trickling into camp just as the scents of lunch were reaching a peak. Behind me, the camp was filling up. The babble of friendly banter washed over me as nobles, soldiers and servants prepared for the meal. No one noticed me. I was slightly hidden by the papyrus stands, so I stayed put, enjoying my false solitude, idly tossing my spear at passing fish.

Suddenly, shouting and the enraged bellows of an animal shattered the river's peace. I froze in place, then one of the Medjay pelted through the papyrus stands past me. He was covered in mud and breathing hard. He ran straight to

Djedmose and saluted. "Sir! That idi–"He caught sight of prince Rekhi-mi-re and changed course. "Sir! Priest Setnacht has wounded a hippopotamus and it has charged him. He's injured but he'll live. The Medjay have engaged it, but–"

There was more splashing, a closer shout and another enraged bellow. Heart in my throat, I swiveled to see a blood-ied hippo charging along the same path the soldier had run. Several spears hung from its torn hide. It was heading right for me and the crowded camp behind me.

Time slowed as the maddened, bellowing animal bore down on me. Churned-up muddy water smacked against my legs and I knew I was going to die right there. I hardly remember flinging my spear. I mostly remember clenching my eyes shut, waiting for impact.

The impact came from behind, instead. And kept com-ing. Terrible screams filled my ears. I finally breathed again and opened my eyes to realize I was not dead and the screams and back-slapping were coming from the Medjay and camp staff. A frighteningly short distance away, the hippopotamus lay twitching in the water, my fishing spear lodged through its eye. I gulped and sagged. The Medjay closed around me, thankfully shutting out the grisly sight.

We broke camp that night. A physician was called in for Setnacht, who escaped with nothing more serious than a bro-ken arm. Everyone was buzzing with my feat and Neffi never left my side. I got more congratulations and praise than I'd ever had. Even Rekhi-mi-re came by my tent and gave me two jars of the white wine. Me, I just nodded and kept my mouth shut. It was the best way to keep from tossing again –

not that I'd been able to eat anything. I kept seeing the charge and then that twitching animal in the bloody, muddy water.

I was securing the last of my chests and the steward was folding up the wondrous bed when Djedmose came by. He handed me a cup of dark red wine and ordered me to sip it.

I collapsed onto a stool and sipped as ordered, fully expecting it to come back up. It didn't. Instead, a calming warmth spread through me. "Thanks."

"Best thing for the shakes, Scribe. Trust me, we all get them."

"And thanks for not congratulating me, either."

The Nubian laughed. "I'll hold that for later when the shock wears off more, but you did good, anyway."

"I didn't do anything. Everyone is taking that shot as proof of magic or real skill. It wasn't magic or skill. It was luck. Pure. Dumb. Luck."

The Medjay's face hardened. "It wasn't luck, Scribe. I don't want to hear that crap again."

I looked at him, anger flaring. Of all people, I thought Djedmose would understand.

"You *wanted* that hippo." With a knowing grin, the captain slapped me on the back, ordered me to finish the wine and strolled off to shout the journey home to a faster pace.

About the Author

T. Lee Harris is a writer and illustrator. A graduate of Indiana University with a bachelor of fine arts, Harris has put her degree to good use when designing and publishing the Indian Creek Anthology series for the Southern Indiana Writers Group and the Not From Around Here anthology for the Cincinnati Writers Project.

Harris' work has appeared in several print and online venues including untreedreads.com, mystericale.com, the Indian Creek Anthology series and Wildside Press' Cat Tales 2 anthology. Her novella "Winter Wonderland," written for the Black Orchid competition, featuring former FBI agent, Dallas Powell, is available through several electronic venues including Amazon's Kindle store and in hard copy through Amazon's CreateSpace. "Hanukkah Gelt," a short story featuring Josh Katzen, is available through untreedreads.com. Several novels are in the works with settings ranging from ancient Egypt to modern-day Chicago.

www.ingramcontent.com/pod-product-compliance
Lightning Source LLC
Chambersburg PA
CBHW061457170626
46811CB00004B/1547